First Rain

Charlotte Herman   Illustrated by **Kathryn Mitter**

Albert Whitman & Company, Chicago, Illinois

*F*or my cousin Lois Schnitzer, who knows all about granddaughters and rain.
And for my own granddaughters, Leah, Ariella, Shoshi, and Leah Nechama,
who know all about good-byes and hellos.

Thank you to my daughters Debbie and Karen for joining me
on my trip to Israel through the writing of this book.—C.H.

Library of Congress Cataloging-in-Publication Data

Herman, Charlotte.
First rain / by Charlotte Herman ; illustrated by Kathryn Mitter.
p. cm.
Summary: When Abby moves with her family to Israel, where it does not rain
all summer, she misses her grandmother and remembers the fun they used to
have splashing in puddles together.
ISBN 978-0-8075-2454-1
[1. Moving, Household—Fiction. 2. Grandmothers—Fiction. 3. Americans—Israel—Fiction.
4. Israel—Fiction. 5. Rain and rainfall—Fiction. 6. Jews—Fiction.] I. Mitter, Kathy, ill.
II. Title.
PZ7.H4313Fir 2010 [E]—dc22 2009023903

The design is by Carol Gildar.
The illustrations are done in acrylic paint on Bristol board.

For more information about Albert Whitman & Company,
please visit our web site at www.albertwhitman.com.

*E*very year, Jewish people move to Israel by the planeloads. In Hebrew, this move is called *aliyah* (ah-lee-AH). They come from countries all over the world, often leaving loved ones behind, to fulfill their dream of living in this ancient land.

In this story, Abby arrives with her parents in the summertime. In Israel during the summer it doesn't rain. You can have a birthday party or other celebrations outside and never have to worry about the rain chasing you back inside.

But after a hot, dry summer, the people of Israel welcome the rain. Children run outside to dance and play in the rain. Rain means water. Water for drinking. Water for crops, and plants, and flowers, and all living things. There is even a prayer for rain.

In Israel—a country both modern and rich in history—Abby will have new experiences. She'll visit new places, eat new foods, and learn a new language.

She'll have all kinds of adventures in the land she now calls home.

*A*bby was in tears. Her mother and father were in tears. And so was Grandma.

They were at the airport where Abby and her parents would soon be flying off to Israel—a country where they had always dreamed of living.

"I wish you were coming with us," said Abby.

"I wish you were staying here," said her grandmother. "Israel is so far away! Even the day is sad that you're leaving. It's been raining all morning."

Grandma took an envelope out of her purse and handed it to Abby. "A plane letter," she said. "Something for you to read when you're up in the air."

There were hugs and kisses, and all too soon they said their good-byes. And Grandma went home. Alone.

Holding the letter tightly, Abby boarded the plane with her parents.
The plane was huge, and packed with people, all of them going to live in Israel.
She sat down and placed Foo Foo Monkey next to her. Then she looked out the
window at the pouring rain—rain she would not see again all summer, since it
didn't rain in Israel in the summertime. And she thought about Grandma.
When would she see her again?

When the plane was up in the air,
Abby read the letter.

Dear Abby,
You are off on a brand new adventure.
You'll meet new people and see new places.
And you'll learn to speak Hebrew, the
language of Israel. So far, I know just one
Hebrew word. Shalom. The word that means
hello, good-bye, and peace.
I wish you a safe and happy trip. I'll
miss you very much, but I'll keep you in
my heart always.
Love, Grandma

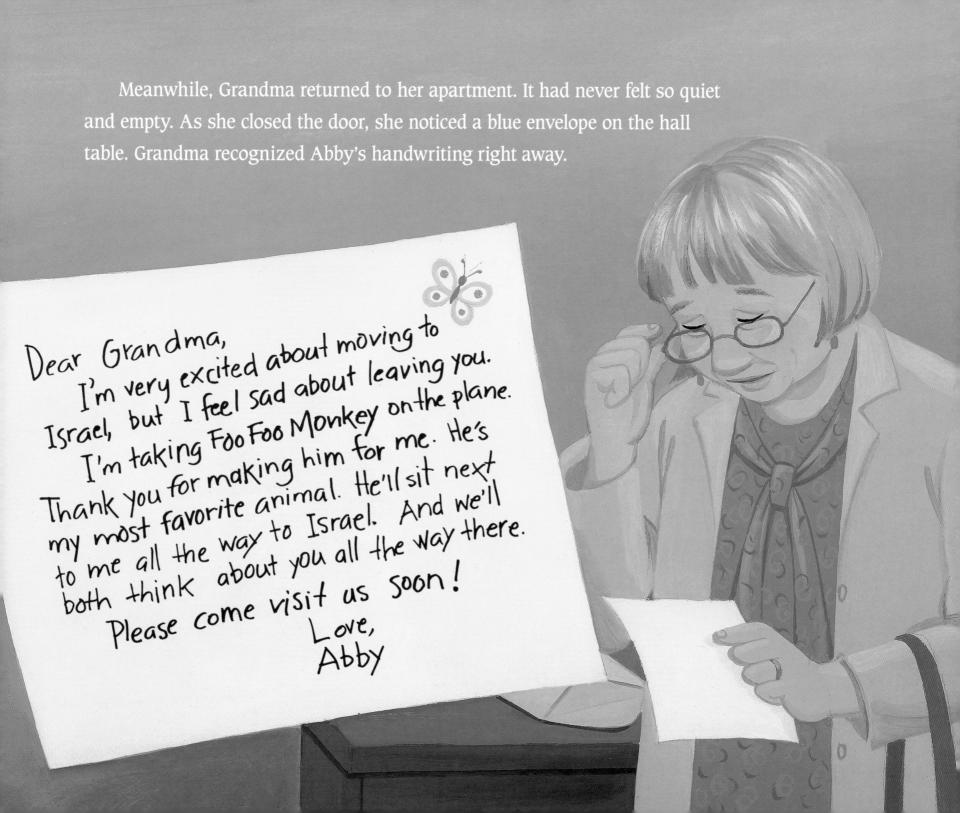

Meanwhile, Grandma returned to her apartment. It had never felt so quiet and empty. As she closed the door, she noticed a blue envelope on the hall table. Grandma recognized Abby's handwriting right away.

Dear Grandma,
    I'm very excited about moving to Israel, but I feel sad about leaving you. I'm taking Foo Foo Monkey on the plane. Thank you for making him for me. He's my most favorite animal. He'll sit next to me all the way to Israel. And we'll both think about you all the way there. Please come visit us soon!
        Love,
        Abby

After her long flight, Abby's Israel adventure began. She and her parents finally arrived at Ben Gurion Airport near Tel Aviv. Abby was surprised by the cheering crowds who came to greet them. Hebrew music was playing, and Israeli flags were waving.

People were laughing and hugging. Abby found herself laughing along with them, and she and her mother and father began hugging each other, too.

Later at her new house, Abby made her first
phone call from Israel.

"Hi, Grandma, we're here! And guess what? I think
the whole country of Israel met us at the airport.
And you know what else? We have a pomegranate tree
right in our backyard. An olive tree, too. And we just
had an Israeli breakfast of cheese and vegetables.
And Foo Foo Monkey says hi."

"Hi, back," said Grandma. "It all sounds wonderful. And I can't get over the fact that you just had breakfast and I'm getting ready to go to sleep."

"Have a good night, Grandma," said Abby.

"Have a good day," said Grandma. "Love you!"

Over the next weeks, Abby and Grandma spoke on the phone and sent letters and emails back and forth. Abby wrote about her visit to Jerusalem and the Western Wall.

"It was amazing, Grandma.
I actually touched the wall that once
surrounded the ancient Temple.
It's over two thousand years old!"

She told how she went on a *tiyul*—a hike *("Now you know two Hebrew words, Grandma")*, explored caves, and waded through a rocky stream.

"You should have seen those rocks, Grandma. They were huge! And the water felt so cool on my feet. I especially enjoyed it because it's been so hot lately. I can't wait for the rain to start.

"Oh—and I have to tell you about the day Mom and I went to the marketplace—
the shuk (your third Hebrew word, Grandma), in Jerusalem. You should have seen it.
There were crowds of shouting people, buying and selling—fruits and vegetables,
sacks of nuts and spices, and candy. I've never seen so many colors or smelled such a
mix of smells in one place! At a fruit stand, Mom and I bought a bag full of the freshest
figs and dates I've ever eaten."

One day a package for Grandma arrived in the mail. Along with the package came a letter from Abby. *"Here is a present for you,"* she wrote. Before Grandma even finished the letter, she opened the package and found a jar of . . . mud. Mud? What kind of present is that? Grandma wondered, and then she went on to read the rest of the letter.

We took a trip to the Dead Sea.
Guess what? You can't sink in the
Dead Sea! I even saw a man
floating on his back and reading
a book. It was so funny!
Just before we left the Dead Sea
I bought a jar and filled it with mud
for you. Dead Sea mud is supposed to
be good for your skin. I hope
you enjoy it.
Until next time...
Abby

Abby sent Grandma photos of the family riding camels,
and of her and her friends at a shopping mall,
eating pizza and falafel.

Grandma sent a photo of her face
covered with the mud from the Dead Sea.

One day Abby called Grandma and said, "Hi, *Savta*."

"Savta?" Grandma asked.

"Yeah. That's Hebrew for Grandma."

"Oh, good. Now I know four words."

"My friend Shira speaks to me in Hebrew and she wants me to speak to her in Hebrew, too. So I'm learning fast."

"I'm happy that things are working out so well for you," Grandma told her. "I thought of you yesterday when it rained. And I wished I could send some of it to you."

"Grandma, remember how on rainy days we used to put on our yellow slickers and our boots? Then we'd take umbrellas and go out in the rain and splash in the puddles!"

"We looked like two yellow ducks!" said Grandma.

Abby burst out laughing, and Grandma
laughed with her.

Grandma was still laughing even
after she hung up the phone.

The long summer days had come to an end. Grandma sent Abby an envelope filled with red and gold autumn leaves from the maple tree outside her apartment building. Abby was in her new school, making more new friends. And she was still waiting for the first rain of the season. Just as she used to wait for the first snow when she lived in America.

Then early one morning Abby woke up to a strange sound.
Something was going *ping ping ping* on the roof of her house.
Could it be?

She ran to the window and
looked out. Yes, yes, yes! It was raining!
The first rain. It rained on the rooftops.
It rained on the sidewalks. It rained on the olive tree
and the pomegranate tree.

Abby hurried to get dressed. Then she put on her rain boots and yellow slicker, grabbed her umbrella, and ran to the door.

And when she opened it, standing there in the rain with a suitcase and an umbrella and wearing a yellow slicker, was Grandma!

They both dropped their umbrellas. Grandma let go of her suitcase, and they fell into each other's arms. They were laughing and crying at the same time. And when the laughing and crying were over, they dried their eyes and picked up their umbrellas.

And the two yellow ducks went out into the rain.

Immigrating to Israel – Making *Aliyah*

At the heart of *First Rain* is a family's move to Israel. For many Jews, residing in the Jewish homeland has special meaning; for them, this move can feel like "coming home" and is known as "making *aliyah*" (from Hebrew, meaning "ascend"). In this contemporary story, Abby's family is clearly making *aliyah* to fulfill personal aspirations; over the centuries, however, many Jews have relocated to Israel because of anti-Semitism or even expulsion from their home country.

A prime example of *aliyah* comes from the book of Genesis, when our patriarch Abraham and his family journeyed to live in the Land of Canaan. Immigrants to Israel – called *olim* in Hebrew – have been arriving ever since, often in great numbers. Waves of immigration have occurred through the centuries, often at times of persecution. One example of mass immigration to Israel is Operation Magic Carpet (1949-50) when nearly the entire population of 49,000 Yemenite Jews was airlifted to Israel: most of those people had never seen an airplane, yet believed the prophecy from the Book of Isaiah that the children of Israel would return "on wings." Another astonishing instance of concentrated immigration occurred with Operation Solomon when, on a single day in 1991, 14,325 Jews were transported to Israel from Ethiopia.

In addition to those mentioned above, Jews from India, France, and the former Soviet Union – to name a few – have made *aliyah* in large numbers. A variety of Israeli organizations now exists to assist these new residents – a significant number of whom are children – helping them learn Hebrew, find work and housing, and adjust to a new and sometimes very different life. For Abby, a home in Israel brought new experiences, new sites, new foods, a new language, and, after a long, dry summer, a delightful walk with her grandmother in the season's first rain.

About The PJ Library®

The PJ Library is an award-winning program brought to you through the generosity of your local Jewish community in partnership with local philanthropists and the Harold Grinspoon Foundation. The PJ Library sends out high-quality Jewish children's books and music to families across North America on a monthly basis. The PJ Library helps families explore the timeless core values of Judaism and transmit these values to a new generation through the closeness of parents and children reading together. To learn more about this exciting initiative, visit www.pjlibrary.org or contact your local Jewish community PJ Library office.